Disney's
POCAHONTAS
The Sparkling River

MOUSE WORKS

As the golden sun rose high over the Indian huts, Pocahontas and her friends Meeko and Flit set off in their canoe. "The river changes every day," Pocahontas said as she paddled downstream. "I can't wait to see what we're going to find."

A fish flipped up beside their canoe, waving hello with it's tail. "Careful, Meeko," Pocahontas warned as the silly raccoon leaned over to wave back. But it was too late—he flopped into the water with a loud SPLASH!

Pocahontas pointed to a patch of sunflowers blooming on the riverbank. "Don't they smell wonderful?" she asked. But, when Flit flew in for a closer sniff, he got his beak stuck inside!

Meeko wondered what the tall green grasses growing in the water were. "They're river reeds," said Pocahontas, as she picked one. "And they're just right for tickling furry tummies!"

Flit flew past a group of fluttering butterflies. They quickly
caught up to the little bird, thinking that Flit was one of them.
Until Flit's humming gave him away!

Under a tree, colorful autumn leaves covered the ground.
"Are you thinking what I'm thinking?" Pocahontas asked.
"Race you to it!" With a running start and a big leap,
Pocahontas was the first to land in the leaves.

"Listen," said Pocahontas as the silver rain landed with a DRIP-DROP.
Flit spread his wings as wide as he could, trying to cover his friends.
"The rain makes the trees and flowers grow," giggled Pocahontas.
"Maybe it'll make Flit's wings grow, too!"

When the rain stopped, a beautiful rainbow appeared. "Look at all the colors of the sky!" Pocahontas said, pulling the canoe onto the shore. "This is a wonderful place to spend the night."

At the end of the day, Pocahontas, Meeko, and Flit sat watching the beautiful night sky. "What treasures the river showed us today," Pocahontas sighed. "And who knows what we'll find tomorrow."

Then, as the stars twinkled in the sky above,
the three friends drifted off to a cozy sleep.